D0265200

Classic Fairytales

CINDERELLA

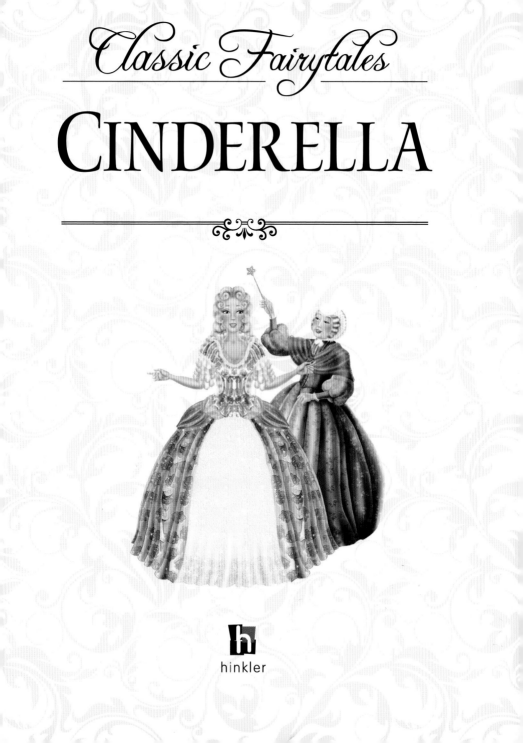

hinkler

This book belongs to

....

CINDERELLA

First published in 2011
by Hinkler Books Pty Ltd
45–55 Fairchild Street
Heatherton Victoria 3202 Australia
www.hinkler.com.au

hinkler

© Hinkler Books Pty Ltd 2011

Editor: Louise Coulthard
Cover Design: Hinkler Design Studio
Cover Illustration: Anton Petrov
Illustrator: Melissa Webb
Prepress: Graphic Print Group

Images © Shutterstock.com: floral background © OnFocus;
decorative border © JungleOutThere; floral silhouette © Leo_RGB;
vintage frame © Ela Kwasniewski

All rights reserved. No part of this publication may be utilised in any
form or by any means electronic or mechanical, including photocopying,
recording or by any information storage or retrieval system now know or
hereafter invented, without the prior written permission of the publishers.

ISBN 978 1 7418 4147 3

Printed and bound in China

Contents

Introduction

The tradition of fairytales and folklore is one that has been with us for centuries. Fairytales are found in every culture and often surprisingly similar stories will have developed on different sides of the world. Regardless of their origins, fairytales can be happy or sad; frightening or reassuring; dark or light; or all of these at once.

The common thing that binds all fairytales together is that they are about the emotions, fears, joys, hopes and dreams that we all share. Whether the fears are expressed through an encounter with a fearsome witch or the joys are found in a princess re-awakened, fairytales touch on feelings and experiences that we can all relate to. Everyone is searching for their very own 'happily ever after'.

The *Classic Fairytales* series presents classic tales from a range of fairytale traditions, be it the scholarly works of the German Brothers Grimm, the tradition of British folk stories, the imagination of Dane Hans Christian Andersen or the courtly tales of Frenchman Charles Perrault. Whatever the source, these fairytales are a much-loved part of growing up and learning about the joys and perils of the world.

Everyone has their own version of their favourite tales. The stories in this series have tried to stay as close to the original versions as possible, but everyone has a different way of telling them. We hope you enjoy our versions. Share them as a family and discover the joys and rewards of reading together.

*O*nce upon a time there lived a gentleman with his young daughter. His wife had passed away, but their daughter had inherited her mother's rare goodness and sweetness of temper.

After several years had passed, the gentleman decided to marry again. Unhappily, his choice of bride was a poor one, for the lady he married was the proudest and most haughty woman imaginable. She had two daughters of her own, who were like her in every way.

The wedding was barely over when the woman's temper began to show. She could not bear the sweetness of the young girl, as it made her own daughters seem even worse. The stepmother gave her the dirtiest, hardest work in the house to do. Every day, she had to scour the dishes, clean the tables, polish the grates, scrub the floors and dust the bedrooms.

The poor girl was forced to sleep in the cold, bare attic on a pile of straw, while her two stepsisters slept in luxurious beds in fine bedrooms lined with mirrors so they could see their fine clothes. The young girl only had a plain shabby cotton dress to wear.

The girl bore all this patiently and did not even complain to her father, who was completely ruled by his wife, as she did not wish to add to his unhappiness. When her work was done, she would sit in the corner next to the chimney among the cinders. Her stepsisters mocked her and called her 'Cinderella'. However, despite her poor clothes and her daily toil, Cinderella was a hundred times more lovely than her stepsisters, despite their fine clothes.

It came to pass that the king's son came of age. A grand ball was announced in his honour and the most important and fashionable people in the town were invited. When their invitation arrived, the stepsisters immediately busied themselves with choosing their gowns, petticoats and jewellery for the occasion. Poor Cinderella spent her days lacing corsets, ironing dresses, picking up discarded clothes, sewing and shopping. The sisters instructed her to style their hair and paint their faces in different ways to see what looked best.

On the night of the ball, Cinderella busily dressed the stepsisters. They taunted her, saying, 'Cinderella, don't you wish that you were going to the ball?'

'Ah, you are laughing at me,' Cinderella sighed. 'It is not for such as I to think about going to balls.'

'You are right,' the stepsisters replied. 'How people would laugh to see a cinder wench dancing at a ball!'

With that, the two stepsisters climbed into their fine carriage and drove off to the ball. Cinderella watched until they were out of sight, and then sat in her corner next to the chimney and burst into tears.

Suddenly a kindly little old lady appeared out of nowhere in front of Cinderella, who was so startled that she stopped crying.

'Dear Cinderella, I am your godmother,' said the woman, who was a fairy. 'Why are you crying? Is it because you wish you could go to the ball?'

'Yes, indeed Godmother!' exclaimed Cinderella.

'Well, do what I say and I shall send you there,' said the fairy godmother. 'But first, I must get you ready. Run to the garden and fetch me a pumpkin.'

Cinderella ran out the kitchen door and soon came back with the largest pumpkin she could find. Her fairy godmother laid it on the ground and tapped it with her wand. The simple pumpkin turned into a beautiful coach made of the finest gold.

Next, the fairy godmother looked in the mousetrap in the pantry and saw that six mice were caught there, poking their noses through the bars. As she freed each mouse, the fairy tapped it with her wand. Each mouse turned into a handsome coach horse, with an elegant long neck, a sweeping tail and a lovely mouse-grey coat.

Then the fairy directed Cinderella to the garden, where she found six lizards. They were soon transformed into six footmen, all wearing shining green and silver coats.

Finally, Cinderella was sent to look in the rat trap. She returned with a great rat with a long beard. One wave of the fairy godmother's wand and the rat turned into a jolly coachman with the finest whiskers imaginable.

'Well my dear, is this equipage fit for the ball?' asked the fairy godmother.

'Why yes!' exclaimed Cinderella. Then she paused and looked down at her shabby, dirty dress. 'But must I go as I am, wearing these rags?'

The fairy godmother touched Cinderella with her wand. Cinderella's shabby dress changed into a beautiful ball gown of gold and silver that sparkled with diamonds. On her feet she wore dainty slippers made of perfect glass.

'Now, my dear, you can go to the ball,' said the fairy godmother. 'Just remember one thing. You must leave before the clock strikes midnight, otherwise your dress will become rags again, your carriage a pumpkin, your horses mice, your footmen lizards and your coachman a rat.'

Cinderella promised she would leave before midnight and then climbed into her coach and drove away, her heart full of joy.

When she arrived at the ball, the whole palace was
struck with how beautiful she was. As soon as he saw her,
the prince was in love. He came forward and lead her into the
ballroom and begged her to dance with him the whole evening.
Everyone marvelled at her elegance and grace as she danced
and all the ladies admired Cinderella's fine gown and imagined
how they could have a dress made just like it.

When supper was served, the prince waited on her himself and was so enamoured that he could not eat. Cinderella saw her stepsisters looking at her in admiration, but when she spoke to them, they did not recognise her. Time passed quickly and soon Cinderella heard the clock chiming eleven and three quarters. She quickly made her exit and returned home.

Cinderella told her fairy godmother about her lovely evening and how the prince had begged her to return for the second night of the ball. As she was talking, she heard her stepsisters return home `and ran to meet them, rubbing her eyes as though she had been sleeping.

'If you had been there, you would have seen such a sight!' exclaimed one sister. 'A beautiful princess attended. No one knows who she is but the prince is smitten and would give the world to know her name. How honoured we were when she spoke to us!'

'Oh I would so like to see her,' said Cinderella. 'Could you not lend me a dress so I could attend the ball, just to catch a glimpse?'

'Don't be ridiculous!' snapped the other sister. 'I would not be so silly as to lend my clothes to a cinder maid!' Cinderella was glad, as she had asked in jest and knew that she would be refused.

The next night, the two stepsisters attended the ball and so did Cinderella, dressed even more magnificently. The prince was constantly by her side and Cinderella so enjoyed his company that she did not notice how the time flew by.

Suddenly, Cinderella heard the clock start to strike twelve. She ran from the ballroom as fast as she could. The prince followed but he could not overtake her. As she ran, she left behind one of her glass slippers on the palace stairs. When Cinderella got home, her clothes had returned to rags but she was clutching the other glass slipper.

The stepsisters returned soon after and Cinderella asked them how they had enjoyed the ball and if the mysterious princess had attended. They replied that she had, but when the clock struck twelve, the princess had run from the ballroom in such haste that she had left behind one of her glass slippers. The prince had picked it up and spent the rest of the ball gazing at it, so in love was he.

A few days later, it was proclaimed that the prince would marry whoever could perfectly fit the glass slipper. All the ladies of the court and palace tried on the slipper, but none could fit into it. It was laid upon a silk cushion and taken to all the ladies of the town for them to try, but to no avail.

When it came to the house of the stepsisters, they tried all they could to fit their feet into the slipper. They pushed and shoved and curled their toes, but the slipper was too small and dainty for them.

'Let me try,' said Cinderella.

The two sisters laughed at her and began to tease her, but the courtier who had been sent with the slipper said that he had orders that every woman must try it on. He slipped the slipper on her foot and found that it fitted as perfectly as if it had been made for her.

As the astonished stepsisters looked on, the fairy godmother appeared and waved her wand and they saw before them the beautiful lady from the ball. They threw themselves before Cinderella and begged her to forgive them. Cinderella was so good that she bade them rise and embraced them.

Cinderella was taken to the prince. When he saw her, the prince thought Cinderella was more beautiful than ever and he fell to his knees and asked her to marry him. A few days later they were married and they lived happily ever after.

The End

Notes for the Reader

Cinderella is one of the most classic, popular fairytales. Variations can be found across many cultures, including China, Korea, Africa, Russia, India, Vietnam, Ireland, Serbia, Germany, Arabia, Scotland, Norway, Italy and Japan. The stories can be traced back to Ancient Greece and Egypt, with the tale *The Girl with the Rose-Red Slippers* thought to be recorded in the 500s BC.

The Grimms' version, *Aschenputtel* (*Ash Girl*), is about a girl who plants a hazel tree on her mother's grave that grants wishes. When she begs to go to the ball, her stepmother throws lentils into the ashes and tells her she may go if she picks them all out. Birds help pick out the lentils, but she is still not permitted to go. The tree grants her wish and she gets her dress. The third time she attends the ball, the prince smears the stairs with pitch to stop her. Her shoe is caught as she runs out. When the stepsisters try the shoe, the first cuts off her toe so the shoe fits, but is caught when blood seeps out. The second cuts off her heel but is also discovered. At the conclusion of the story, the birds peck out the stepsisters' eyes.

Modern readers are most familiar with the version recorded by Frenchman Charles Perrault in his collection *Contes de ma Mere L'Oye* (*Tales of Mother Goose*). This story, called *Cendrillon*, was written in 1697 and saw the appearance of the fairy godmother, the pumpkin carriage and the glass slippers. Perrault's tale was written when fairytales were extremely popular among the wealthy aristocracy and is much less violent than the Grimms' German version. The version in this collection is based on the Perrault tale.